Are all houses the same?

Written by Katie Foufouti

Illustrated by Daniela Geremia

Collins

What's in this book?

Listen and say

stairs

fire

Download the audio at www.collins.co.uk/839764

ice

bridge

light

Daddy says, "Look at all the houses, Joy. Can you see our house?"

4

Joy says, "No, I can't.
Are all houses the same?"

Look at this house! It's in a tree.

tree house

The family walk on a bridge to their house.

In this house, there's a bed and
a kitchen.

It's a small house and you can drive it!

motorhome

This boat is a house, too.
It's a houseboat!

houseboat

Look! It's got a fire in the living room.

You can make a house with ice.

ice house

Is it cold in the ice house? No, it isn't!

These people live in cave houses.

cave houses

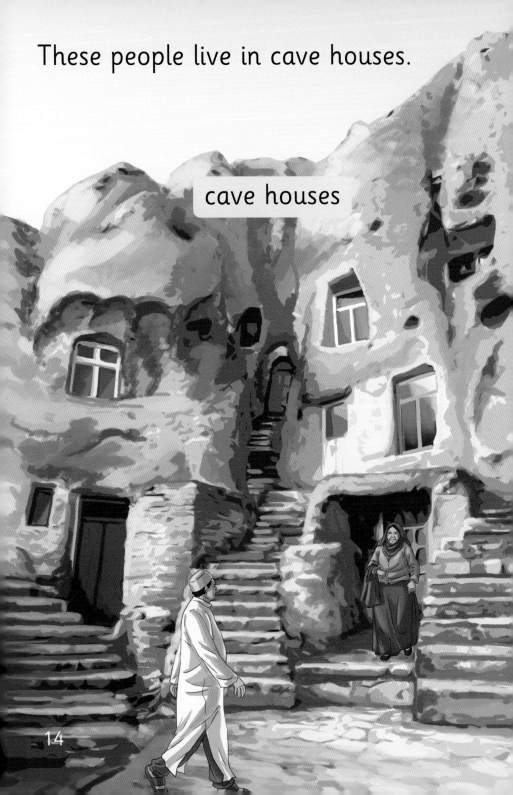

This is the living room. It's very nice!

There are lots of stairs in this house.

This house has a big light. Ships can see the light at night.

big light

lighthouse

17

Look! The sea is under this house!

stilt house

stilt

You can swim and catch fish from this house.

Joy says, "There are lots of different houses."

Picture dictionary

Listen and repeat

cave house

houseboat

ice house

lighthouse

motorhome

stilt house

tree house

1 Look and match

The sea is under this house.

You can drive this house.

This house has a big light.

2 Listen and say

Collins

Published by Collins
An imprint of HarperCollins*Publishers*
Westerhill Road
Bishopbriggs
Glasgow
G64 2QT

HarperCollins*Publishers*
1st Floor, Watermarque Building
Ringsend Road
Dublin 4
Ireland

William Collins' dream of knowledge for all began with the publication of his first book in 1819.

A self-educated mill worker, he not only enriched millions of lives, but also founded a flourishing publishing house. Today, staying true to this spirit, Collins books are packed with inspiration, innovation and practical expertise. They place you at the centre of a world of possibility and give you exactly what you need to explore it.

© HarperCollins*Publishers* Limited 2020

10 9 8 7 6 5 4 3 2

ISBN 978-0-00-839764-7

Collins® and COBUILD® are registered trademarks of HarperCollins*Publishers* Limited

www.collins.co.uk/elt

British Library Cataloguing in Publication Data

A catalogue record for this publication is available from the British Library.

Author: Katie Foufouti
Illustrator: Daniela Geremia (Beehive)
Series editor: Rebecca Adlard
Commissioning editor: Zoë Clarke
Publishing manager: Lisa Todd
Product managers: Jennifer Hall and Caroline Green
In-house editor: Alma Puts Keren
Project manager: Emily Hooton
Editor: Barbara MacKay
Proofreaders: Natalie Murray and Michael Lamb
Cover designer: Kevin Robbins
Typesetter: 2Hoots Publishing Services Ltd
Audio produced by id audio, London
Reading guide author: Emma Wilkinson
Production controller: Rachel Weaver
Printed and bound by: GPS Group, Slovenia

Download the audio for this book and a reading guide for parents and teachers at www.collins.co.uk/839764